THE JOURNEY THROUGH TIME

Scholastic Inc.

Library of Congress Cataloging-in-Publication Data Available

ISBN 978-0-545-55623-1

Based on an original idea by Elisabetta Dami.

www.geronimostilton.com

Published by Scholastic Inc., 557 Broadway, New York, NY 10012. SCHOLASTIC and associated logos are trademarks and/or registered trademarks of Scholastic Inc.

Stilton is the name of a famous English cheese. It is a registered trademark of the Stilton Cheese Makers' Association. For more information, go to www.stiltoncheese.com.

Text by Geronimo Stilton
Original title *Viaggio nel tempo*
Cover by Silvia Bigolin (pencils and inks) and Christian Aliprandi (color)
Illustration concepts by Lorenzo Chiavini, Blasco Pisapia, Roberto Ronchi, and Valeria Turati
Illustration production by Silvia Bigolin, Danilo Barozzi, Valeria Brambilla, Giuseppe Guindani (pencils and inks), Christian Aliprandi (color), and Francesco Barbieri
Graphics by Merenguita Gingermouse, Zeppola Zap, and Yuko Egusa with Chiara Cebraro and Studio Editoriale Littera

Special thanks to AnnMarie Anderson
Translated by Lidia Morson Tramontozzi
Interior design by Kay Petronio

13 12 11 10 9   18 19 20 21 22/0

Printed in China   38

First printing, January 2014

TRAVELERS ON
THE JOURNEY THROUGH TIME

Dear rodent friends,
My name is Stilton, *Geronimo Stilton*. I am
the editor and publisher of <u>The Rodent's Gazette</u>,
the most famous newspaper on Mouse Island.
I'm about to tell you the story of one of my most
amazing adventures. Let me introduce you to the
other mice you will meet. . . .

THEA STILTON

My sister, Thea, is a special correspondent for
The Rodent's Gazette. She is very athletic and
one of the most stubborn and determined
mice I have ever met!

BENJAMIN

My nephew Benjamin is the
sweetest and most affectionate
little mouselet in the whole world.

TRAP

My cousin Trap is an incredible
prankster. His favorite pastime
is playing jokes on me.

PROFESSOR PAWS VON VOLT

Professor von Volt is a genius inventor
who has dedicated his life to making
amazing new discoveries. This time,
he built a time machine!

THE MYSTERIOUS LETTER

It was a FOGGY December morning. I left home, got a coffee at a nearby café, and munched on a **cheesy** croissant as I leafed through my newspaper, *The Rodent's Gazette*, while walking to work. Five minutes later, I was in my office.

I immediately noticed a **mysterious** letter sitting on my desk. The envelope was **sealed** with a yellow wax stamp with a peculiar symbol on it: a **QUESTION MARK**.

The handwriting looked **very** familiar to me. I opened the

Geronimo Stilton

envelope cautiously. A **rusty** key slipped out along with a sheet of **crumbly** old notepaper that smelled like **moldy** cheese.

Intrigued, I read the note.

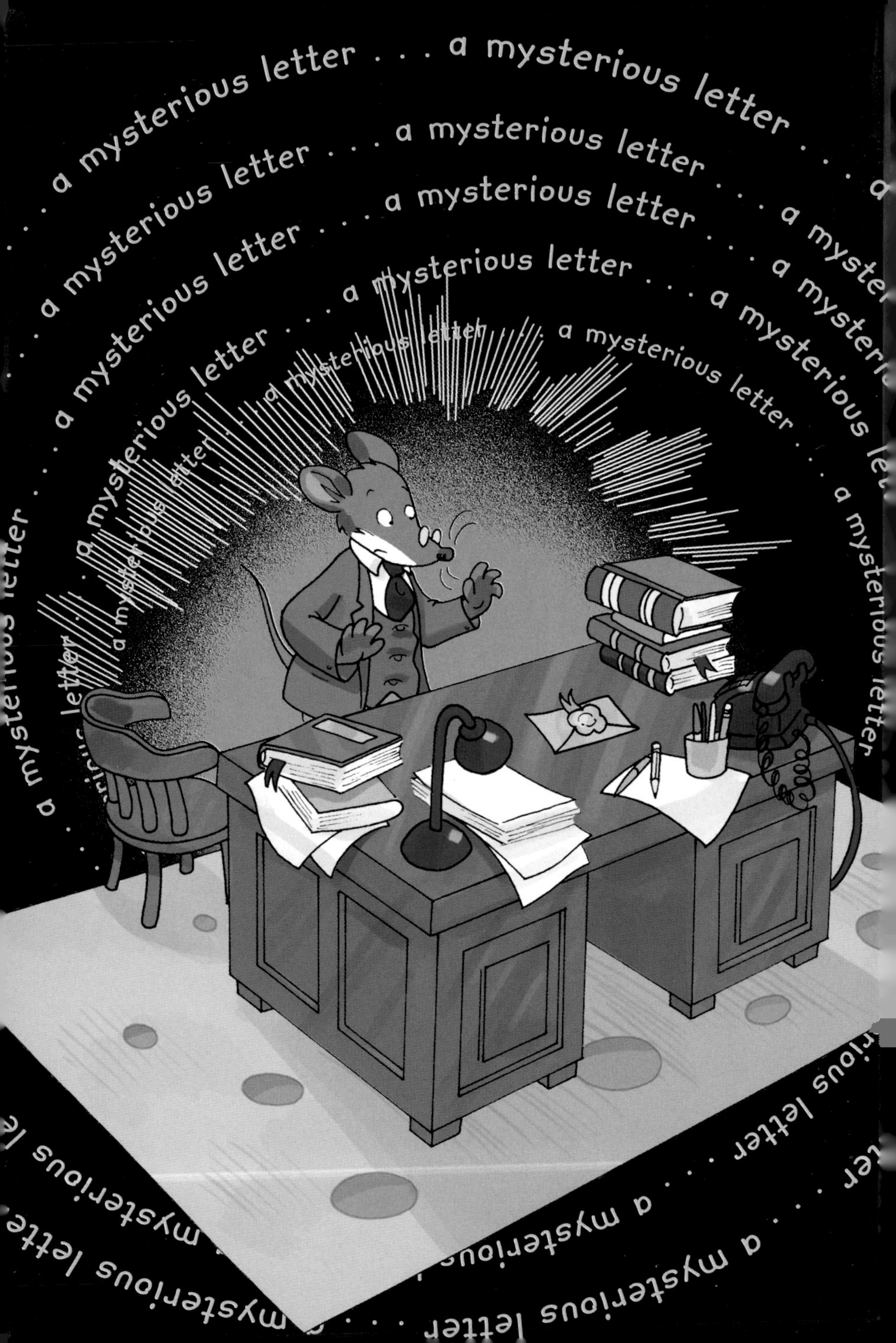
a mysterious letter . . .

Geronimo!

Take the number 17 trolley from Romano Square and get off at the seventh stop. Walk to the traffic light, then take the second street on the left, then the third on the right, and then the first on the left. Cross the bridge, take twenty-three-and-a-half steps, until you reach the billboard with the Gorgonzola cheese ad. Then take fourteen steps toward the telephone booth. You should find yourself standing in front of a clock. Turn your back to the clock and take seven steps toward the pizzeria. Go inside the pizzeria, walk to the bathroom, exit through the small window, and climb over the low wall.

Now walk for exactly thirty seconds toward the shoe store, go around the corner, and continue walking until you see a little black door with a sign on it that says DO NOT ENTER. *Open the door using the enclosed key. Go through the door, and you'll find yourself in an alley. Take the first right, then the second left, then the third right. Turn into a yard and proceed until you reach a large Dumpster. Climb into the Dumpster for an amazing adventure!*

Signed,
??????

P.S. Commit these instructions to memory, then destroy the letter! Do not talk about this to anyone! It's an extremely secretive secret!

"Moldy mozzarella!" I squeaked. "An **adventure** in a Dumpster? What an **intriguing** letter!"

I carefully reread the letter and examined it with a **magnifying glass**.

"Hmmm," I said to myself. "It *could* be a prank, but if it's not . . ."

I thought about it for a minute as my whiskers **trembled** with excitement. Then I made my decision. I memorized the instructions, tore the letter into a thousand pieces, and without saying anything to anyone, quietly slipped out of the office. I **scampered** to the corner, crossed the street, and ran to catch the **number 17** trolley.

MY WHISKERS
TREMBLED . . .

The trolley was very, very **CROWDED**. I pushed my way through rats and mice on their way to work. I looked out the window. A dusting of fresh **snow** covered the streets of New Mouse City, and it was truly **BEAUTIFUL**! The rooftops looked like white pillows, while the **ice** made the trees look like they were dressed for a party in delicate *lace*.

Lost in thought, I almost didn't notice the trolley had come to the seventh stop. The doors creaked open. **Creak! Creak!**

I stepped off the trolley to find that the **FOG** had gotten thicker. I couldn't see anything beyond my own paw! I cleaned my fogged glasses and tried to remember the instructions in the **MYSTERIOUS** letter.